MURRAY'S NIGHTMARE

Janet Lorimer

PAGETURNERS

Development and Production: Laurel Associates, Inc.
Cover Illustrator: Black Eagle Productions

SADDLEBACK
EDUCATIONAL PUBLISHING

Three Watson
Irvine, CA 92618-2767

Website: www.sdlback.com

ISBN-13: 978-1-56254-133-0
ISBN-10: 1-56254-133-1
eBook: 978-1-60291-235-9

Printed in the United States of America
11 10 09 08   9 8 7 6 5 4 3 2

CONTENTS

Chapter 1

Rita Murray dug around in her jeans pocket for a piece of candy, but all she found was an empty wrapper. She knew that people weren't supposed to eat in the library, of course. But today Rita was willing to break the rules. Her stomach was growling!

Then she remembered. She'd gotten rid of all her candy. That was Monday, when she'd started the New-U diet. Rita groaned softly. She was hungry enough to eat a library book! But then she thought about the two pounds she'd lost in just a few days. She sighed. The diet seemed to be working—but was it worth it to always feel hungry?

"Hungry? More like *starved*," Rita muttered. She stared at the book she was holding, but the print seemed to blur. Could a person go *blind* from hunger? Rita sighed and tried to focus on her studies.

"Hush!" The word came out too loud and seemed to echo back from every corner of the library.

Rita glanced up, expecting to see other students glaring at her. But no one was paying any attention. At one table, a petite redheaded cheerleader named Bambi was flirting with a quarterback. Bambi and Rita lived on the same floor of the dorm. For some reason Bambi loved to bait Rita. Rita had never been able to figure out what she'd done to become Bambi's target.

At another table, two nerds were buried in a pile of computer printouts. Other students worked on papers or hunted in the stacks for books. No one seemed to have noticed that Rita Murray was talking to herself.

Lately, she thought she was hearing

sounds that weren't there. "Next thing you know, I'll be *seeing* things," Rita muttered unhappily.

Rita glanced around again and saw a couple of students looking at her. This time they *had* heard her! She really must get over the bad habit of talking to herself out loud.

Rita had always tried to laugh it off. She'd say that she talked to herself because she was her own best friend—but she knew it was just an excuse. The fact was, she really didn't have a lot of friends. When she'd started college last year, she'd met a few other girls who were also—well, girls who had weight problems. But other than size, she really had nothing in common with them. She didn't want to hang around with them. On the other hand, she had nothing in common with girls like Bambi, either.

"I need to change my image," Rita thought. Those were the words she said to herself over and over, day after day.

I need to change my image.

That was easier said than done. Oh, sure, she could go to the campus fitness center and exercise. But somehow that always seemed to be more trouble than it was worth. Instead, she found herself watching aerobic workouts on TV while she ate lunch. Sometimes she borrowed a stack of her roommate's fashion magazines, hoping the glossy photos would inspire her. The models were so beautiful with their long legs and lean bodies! Every one of them had perfect makeup, hair, and clothes.

"I wonder if models ever get zits," Rita thought with a heavy sigh.

She gazed at the title of the book she was trying so hard to read. It was about Tibet. At first, choosing Tibet as the subject for a paper on art in native costumes had seemed like a great idea. She really enjoyed reading about the people of Tibet—their culture and history. Then she'd gone on this stupid diet. Now, what with the hunger pangs and all, she could barely make it through a single page of the book!

Rita sighed and thumbed through the pages, looking at the photos of Tibetan women in their native dress. "I wonder if *they* ever get zits or go on diets," Rita thought.

The Tibetan women seemed to smile at Rita out of the photographs. Their intelligent faces looked as if they had more important things to think about.

I need to change my image! Rita began doodling while she thought about her image. *If I could change myself* . . . She sketched a girl with long legs. *If I could make myself over* . . . Long dark hair that swirled out like a shimmering curtain of silk. A strong upper body.

"Wow! What a babe!" The voice, not five inches away, startled Rita. Without meaning to, she yelped.

"*Hush!*" This time the voice was real—and so were the frowns from the other students in the reading room. Rita glanced in Bambi's direction. The redhead glared at her, and Rita felt herself blushing.

Then she in turn glared at the young man who was leaning over her shoulder and gazing at the drawing. Gary Stine was one of Rita's few good friends. He wasn't really a handsome guy, but she liked Gary a lot. She liked his sense of humor and his bright mind.

"You scared me," she whispered hoarsely.

Gary grinned, dropping into a chair across the table from her. "Hey, Murray, I thought you were supposed to be writing a paper? Or does this one come with woman warrior illustrations?"

"Very funny!" Rita crumpled up the drawing. She hated it when Gary called her by her last name. But he always did that when he wanted to tease her.

"Don't toss it out," Gary said. "It's a good drawing. But how does it fit in with your paper on Tibetan costumes?"

Rita decided to change the subject. "Let's go, Gary. Are you ready to get something to eat?" she asked.

Gary nodded. As Rita stuffed her books and papers into her backpack, he asked, "So who *is* that babe you were drawing? Is it *you*, by any chance?"

Rita glared at him. "Very funny, Gary. Come on—does she *look* like me?"

"Matter of fact, she does," Gary said. He smoothed out the crumpled drawing. "Yep. You drew *yourself*, Murray."

Startled, she studied the picture. As much as she hated to admit it, Gary was right. She'd drawn her own face, but that was all. The woman's gorgeous build certainly wasn't at all like Rita's. *I need to change my image.*

"You know what I want?" she said. "A double bacon cheeseburger with fries and a chocolate milkshake."

Gary stared at her in amazement. "I thought you were on a diet."

"I didn't say that's what I was going to eat," Rita snapped. "Only what I *wish* I could eat. Will you stop bugging me with stupid questions?"

"I wish you hadn't gone on this crazy diet," Gary said. "You always get so cranky when you're hungry."

"You are such a wimp, Rita Murray!" This time the words really did echo from all four corners of the room.

 **Chapter 2**

Startled, Rita glanced around, but no one looked her way. Then she heard a chuckle and turned around quickly. No one was laughing. "What in the world is wrong with me?" she thought.

Then suddenly, the whole room seemed to sway. Gary grabbed Rita's arm to steady her. "Hey, girl, are you all right?"

Rita closed her eyes. When she opened them again, the room seemed to have stopped moving. "I—I guess I'm really hungry," she croaked weakly.

"Let's get out of here. You need to get some food into you," Gary said.

As they walked out of the library, Rita heard Bambi giggle and sing off-key, "All ya need is love. . . . "

Once they got outside, Rita began to feel better. The library had been hot and stuffy, and the fresh air revived her. "And I'll feel even better when I eat some lunch," she muttered.

"What?" Gary asked.

Rita felt her cheeks growing hot. "Oh, nothing," she said. "I was just thinking out loud. Where are we going?"

"How about the mall?" Gary said. "The walk will do you good. Besides, they've just opened up a new place I want to check out."

"Can you be a little more vague?" Rita said sarcastically. "What kind of place? Are we talking about a shoestore or a hardware store or what?"

Gary made a face at her. "It's a combination virtual reality game shop and fast food joint," he said.

Gary was crazy about computer everything. He was a real wizard when it came to electronics, and he'd been talking for weeks about the great new place about to open up in the mall.

"This is going to be the first in a chain of Triple-E stores," Gary said. "If the concept takes off here, it could spread across the country."

"Making its creators rich and famous," Rita said. "Tell me again, what does Triple-E stand for?"

"Electronic Essential Existence," Gary said with a smile. "That's a fancy way of saying virtual reality."

By now they had reached the mall. The line into the Triple-E store curled outside the door like a dragon's tail.

"We'll never get in," Rita wailed. Now she was ready to abandon the diet *and* Gary. She'd even ditch civilized behavior to get something to eat!

Gary winked at Rita and waved two pieces of paper in front of her nose. She blinked, trying to focus.

"Special passes," he said with a grin. "I promised to write a great review of Triple-E for the campus paper—but only if I got in on opening night. Naturally, the manager couldn't say no!"

Rita had to admit that it felt good to walk to the front of the crowd. What a kick to have the doorman wave you through a line of 100 waiting students! A few minutes later, Rita found herself in a back booth with a plate of food in front of her. So what if it was mostly greasy stuff? At this point, she didn't care. "I'll start my diet again tomorrow," she said, stuffing an onion ring into her mouth.

When the first pangs of hunger were satisfied, Rita took a good look around. "I can see how this place would make money," she told Gary. "Especially being so close to a college campus."

The room was packed with young people. The music was loud, neon signs flashed, and the colors were bold. While customers waited for a turn in a virtual reality booth, there was a lot to do. They could play other electronic games, eat, or just hang out talking with other players.

"What makes this place so different from all the other V-R shops?" Rita asked.

Gary grinned. "A really clever new twist. Here, you get to create a virtual reality partner."

"Huh?" Rita leaned forward, trying to hear him over the blasting music.

Gary raised his voice. "I said you get to design a virtual reality game partner who plays the game with you."

"How?" Rita gazed at him. When he talked to her, Gary always forgot that she didn't know much about electronics.

"It's easy. You—"

Then a loudspeaker bellowed out Gary's name. He climbed out of the booth and grabbed Rita's hand. "Come on," he said excitedly, pulling her to her feet. "It's our turn!"

"What are you talking about?" she asked uneasily.

"We have to test the game booths.

That's why we're here, you know."

"But I don't—"

"Look, it's easy," Gary said. "I'll walk you through every step. Come on."

Rita sighed.

"You are such a wimp, Rita Murray!"

Rita turned quickly. It was the same mocking voice she'd heard in the library! But just as before, no one was paying any attention to her.

"I've eaten," she thought. "Why am I still hearing things?"

Then she heard the chuckle again. "Maybe I'm just stressed out," she thought. "Eating all that rich food after days of eating almost nothing. Maybe my system is over-reacting."

"Rita! You keep saying you want to change your image," the mocking voice continued. *"Well, here's your chance."* Rita looked around in dismay.

"Rita, come on!" Gary jerked her arm impatiently. She took a deep breath and hurried after him.

Gary helped Rita into the headgear and gloves. Then he showed her how to create her virtual reality partner.

"Just follow the directions," he told her. Rita wanted to ask for more help, but she could see that he was anxious to be off to his own booth.

Rita was beginning to feel annoyed with Gary and a little sorry for herself. Then the thought of that mocking voice came back to her. She took a deep breath. "I am *not* a wimp," she thought. "I'll show him!"

Rita did exactly what the recorded voice told her to do. She could choose from a wide selection of already-made-up characters or create her own. Surprisingly, Rita's hand seemed to move by itself. She picked up the electronic pen and began to draw on the computerized pad. There was that girl again—the long legs and lean body with a strong upper torso! And just as before, she had long dark hair that swirled out like a shimmering curtain of silk.

"When you are finished, press *enter*," the recorded voice instructed.

Rita did as she was told and then gasped in astonishment. Someone was standing just a few feet away. Right there in the game booth was her new partner—the woman in her drawing.

Chapter 3

"Now, you must name your game partner." The recorded voice cut through her thoughts. "Now you must name your game partner. Now you must—"

"Okay, *okay*. I get it," Rita said. "But how do I—"

"Say the name of your game partner out loud. Speak slowly and clearly."

"Uh, uh—" Rita's mind went blank.

The lookalike woman beside her gazed at Rita without moving.

"Say the name of—"

"*Rowena!*" Rita yelled. Then she said the name again, this time very slowly. For some reason, she had always liked that name. Somehow it made her think of castles and knights and dragons.

Rowena stirred and seemed to come

to life. She was wearing a black suede outfit—shirt, pants, and thigh-high boots. The clothes fit her to a T. The sleeveless shirt revealed well-defined muscles in her arms. Her long dark hair was held back by a leather thong. The young woman had Rita's features, but her smooth skin glowed. "Boy, does she look healthy!" Rita thought.

"I *am* healthy," Rowena said. "And you would be too if you'd get off that silly diet and get some exercise."

Rita's jaw dropped. "You can talk?"

"Well, of course I can talk," Rowena smiled. She pulled her sword from the sheath that was attached to her belt and touched its sharp edge. "Come on. Are you ready to play?"

All of a sudden, Rita realized that she and Rowena were standing on a path in a virtual forest. Rita could smell the sweet scent of flowers. She could feel the warm grass beneath her feet and hear birds singing in the tree branches. Rita gulped. "Where are we?" she asked.

Rowena smirked playfully and rolled her eyes. "In a forest. *Duh!*"

Rita laughed nervously. That was exactly what she would have said—and in the same sarcastic tone of voice. "You really *are* like me!" she cried out.

Rowena nodded. "That's right. I'm part of you, Rita."

"That's how you knew about my diet," Rita said.

Then she realized how stupid that sounded. Again, she and Rowena both said *"Duh!"* at the same time, and they both burst out laughing.

"This is wild," Rita cried. "It's like having a sister. A virtual twin."

"So, how about it? Are you ready to play?" Rowena asked.

Rita hadn't played many virtual reality games before, so she wasn't sure what to do. Glancing down, she was amazed to see that she, too, was wearing V-R armor. In a sheath at her side was a long sword, the exact duplicate of Rowena's!

"What's the game about?" she asked.

Rowena smiled. "We're on a quest," she said, leading the way down the path. "We have to rescue the sleeping prince who is guarded by a dragon at—"

"I thought the old story was about a sleeping *princess*," Rita said.

Rowena threw back her head and laughed loudly. "Not in this game, honey. We warrior women have to save the poor guy from the evil wizard."

Rita felt as if she were in a dream. Together, she and Rowena fought an army of gnomes. They leaped off a high cliff into a raging river. And they walked a tightrope across a deep dark canyon.

With Rowena at her side, Rita discovered that there was almost *nothing* she couldn't do. Before long, they had chased away the wizard, slain the dragon, and rescued the poor prince. The game was over!

Rita took off the headgear, blinking at the bare walls of the game booth. After all her exciting adventures, she felt a disappointing letdown.

Then the door to the game booth opened and Gary entered. "Well?" He was grinning from ear to ear. "Tell me all about it. Did you have fun?"

Rita just stared at him. He seemed to mistake her sad look for disappointment in the game.

"Didn't you have a good time?" He shook his head. "Aw, too bad, Rita. Tell you what—I'll buy you a hot fudge sundae! Then you can tell me what you thought of the game."

But Rita didn't want hot fudge. She wanted to be back on the cliff hearing Rowena urging her to jump. She wanted to be thrusting her sword through the glittering scales of a green dragon.

"Look, other people are signed up for the booth," Gary said impatiently. "We have to go. It's someone else's turn."

Rita sighed as they left the booth. "I'm not hungry," she said. "It's late. I think we'd better head back to campus."

Gary looked over at her in surprise. "You're turning down hot fudge? I can't believe it. Murray, are you sick?"

Rita had to admit that she felt a little strange. The music in the store beat against her eardrums, and the noise of the crowd rose and fell like waves. The neon lights flashed in rhythm to the music. Rita closed her eyes. Was the *room* swaying, or was she?

Rita reached out to grab hold of Gary just as her knees buckled. The sound and the lights seemed to swirl together in her head. Then everything went black.

Rita felt something cold and wet pressed against her forehead. Then her nose was filled with a stinging odor. She tried to pull back as she heard someone say, "She's coming around."

Her eyes snapped open, and then narrowed against the light. She could see a man dressed like a medic leaning over her. And just behind the medic stood her friend Gary, a worried look clouding his face.

"What happened?" she asked in a weak voice.

"You passed out," Gary said. "Scared me half to death."

"Let's get her into the ambulance," the medic ordered.

"Wait!" Rita yelped. She struggled to sit up and tried to look alert. "Thanks anyway, but I don't need to go to the hospital. I'm *fine*, really. It must have been that stupid diet—"

The medic raised an eyebrow. Then he began asking her questions about her medical history and the diet. Rita felt embarrassed when she told him about what she'd been eating. Or rather, what she *hadn't* been eating.

"A word of advice, Ms. Murray," the medic said when he was certain she was going to be all right. "You'd be smart to stay away from crazy fad diets. They can make you really sick."

Rita sighed. "I know. I just—"

"Any woman who can kill a dragon doesn't need a diet to look terrific!"

There it was again, that familiar mocking voice! But the game was over, wasn't it? "Must be nothing but my imagination," Rita thought.

"Hey, Murray, over here." Now Rita could tell that the mocking voice came from her right. She turned to look and there she was—standing in the crowd. A cocky grin was on her face, and her arms were folded across her chest. It was Rowena!

 **Chapter 4**

Rita squeezed her eyes shut and then opened them. Rowena hadn't budged.

"Are you *sure* you're okay?" the medic asked. He studied Rita's face. "Maybe you should go to the emergency room just to be on the safe side."

"No, no!" Rita insisted. "I—I'm fine. Just a little weak, I guess."

"I'll get her home safe and sound," Gary said, coming forward.

"Your hero to the rescue!" Rowena said with a scornful laugh.

"Gary's not a hero. He's just a good friend," Rita said to Rowena.

With one eyebrow raised, the medic glanced at Gary. Gary's cheeks turned red. "*No*, Gary! I didn't mean—" Rita started to say.

"Sounds to me like a good friend is just what you need," the medic said, as he packed up his stethoscope.

A couple of minutes later, the crowd began to thin out and the ambulance had pulled away. Rowena, too, seemed to have disappeared. Rita felt a sense of relief. She didn't need to be seeing things as well as hearing them.

"What do you think? Do you want me to call a cab?" Gary asked. "Or do you think you feel well enough to walk back to the dorm?"

"I can walk," Rita said. She knew Gary had misunderstood what she'd said to Rowena. Now he looked hurt and embarrassed—and she didn't blame him. But how could she possibly make him understand? Anything she could think of to say would only make matters worse.

They walked in silence for a few minutes. Then Rita said, "I really had a good time this afternoon, Gary."

"Good." Gary's tone was curt. She

glanced sideways. His face was stony, and he was staring straight ahead.

"I—I never liked V-R games before," Rita tried to explain. "But you're right. This V-R shop is different."

"Glad to hear it." Short, curt, and to the point. His jaw was clenched.

"Oh, please don't be mad! I don't know what I was thinking, Gary. Half my mind was still in the game. I guess I was talking to my game partner."

Gary sighed. "Okay. Maybe I can buy that. Sometimes V-R games do seem to be more real than real life."

"Oh, believe me, this one sure did," Rita said. She laughed, feeling as if she were on the edge of hysteria.

"So can I get an exclusive interview with you for my article?" Gary asked with a grin.

Rita smiled and nodded. It was the least she could do.

By now they had reached Rita's dorm. They arranged to meet the next night for dinner. "My treat," Rita said.

"But only on one condition," Gary said seriously. "Promise me you'll get off that maniac diet, okay?"

"Well . . . "

"Good idea! I already told you—you don't need a stupid diet."

It was that voice again! Rita gasped, sneaking a look over Gary's shoulder. Rowena was casually leaning against the wall of the dorm.

Gary frowned. "What?" He glanced over his shoulder and then back at Rita. "What did you see?"

"Uh, nothing!" Rita said quickly. "I, uh—just remembered that I have a quiz on Monday, and I—uh, need to—uh, do some studying tonight!"

Gary shook his head in confusion. "Murray, you are acting so weird!"

Rita laughed nervously. "Am I? I don't mean to." She gazed at Rowena in disbelief. How could this be? How could Rowena still be with her?

Rowena shook her head in disgust. "Come on, Murray, get a grip!"

Without thinking, Rita snapped, "Get out of here!"

"That does it!" Gary glared at Rita. "I'm going, Murray, and you can be sure that I'll never—"

"Not *you*!" Rita yelped. "Oh, Gary, I didn't mean you."

Gary stared at her, his mouth open. "Then who—"

"Uh—uh, I was talking to a—uh, mosquito!" She waved at the air. "Big mosquito."

"Give me a break, Murray, that's *lame*! You'll have to do better than that," Rowena said with a grin.

Gary continued to stare at Rita as if he thought she was out of her mind.

"I'll see you tomorrow night—and consider me off the diet," Rita said quickly. She dashed to the front door and yanked it open. "Thanks again," she called out just as the door slammed behind her. She glanced out the window. Poor Gary! He was standing right where she'd left him, staring through the glass as if she were a visitor from another world.

Rita hurried upstairs. She stood in the shower for a long time, letting the hot water relax her. But somehow she couldn't wash away the memory of her afternoon with Rowena.

"Don't think about her," Rita scolded herself. "Relax! Think about Tibet. Think about costumes. Think about art."

It seemed to work. Rowena didn't appear again. "Maybe she can't get into the building," Rita thought. Then she shook herself to clear her head.

"What am I thinking! She's not *real*. Rowena is make-believe. She's got to be the result of too many onion rings or too little sleep or something."

But what in the world could that *something* be?

Chapter 5

"Get up!"

Rita opened one eye. She was snug in her bed, and the room was dark. A pale green light glowed from the alarm clock on her desk. She must be asleep. This had to be a dream!

"Get up!" It was that voice again. No, it wasn't a dream. It was a nightmare. Then someone grabbed her arm and shook her. Rita blinked, sat up, and fumbled for the lamp. As the light flooded the room, it almost blinded her. She rubbed her eyes.

"Get—"

"*All right!*" Rita roared. Then she saw who was ordering her around. Rowena was frowning down at her. Rita's eyes widened. Suddenly she was no longer sleepy. "How did you get in here?"

Rowena ignored the question. "Hurry up now. Go get dressed. Sweatpants and a sweatshirt will do."

This time Rita lost it. "Just who do you think you are, breaking into my room, ordering me to get up, and telling me what to wear? And while we're on the subject, just where do you think I'm going at—" She glanced at the clock. "Five o'clock? You must be kidding. The civilized world is sound asleep, Rowena. It's *Saturday*, for crying out loud!"

"It's time for you to get to the fitness center," Rowena said. "You need to have some exercise before breakfast."

Rita's jaw dropped in surprise. "You are insane—maybe criminally insane! What you are suggesting is outrageous and—*criminal*. If you think—"

Suddenly the covers flew off the bed, landing in a heap in the far corner of the room. Rowena pulled Rita's clothes out of a drawer and tossed them on the bed.

"Do you need help getting dressed?"

"Hey! You're *not* my mother," Rita snapped. "I am not getting up to—"

A moment later, Rita found herself sitting on the rug. Rowena, hands on hips, was sternly gazing down at her. "Someday you'll thank me, Rita!"

Fifteen minutes later Rita was on her way to the fitness center. A few joggers ran by, but otherwise the campus was quiet at this hour of the morning. Rita took a deep breath of chilly air. It smelled clean and fresh. In the east, the sky was turning rosy. Suddenly Rita realized that she'd never seen the sun rise on campus. Come to think of it, she'd never watched a sunrise *anywhere*!

When she got to the center, Rita discovered that several other students were taking advantage of the early hour to work out. She also realized that she would have to listen to Rowena without talking back. Because no one else could see or hear Rowena, other people looked at Rita oddly when they thought she might be talking to them. "Well, this will certainly cure my bad habit of talking to myself," she thought.

Rowena started Rita walking on the treadmill. Next, Rita rode a stationary bicycle for several sweaty miles. After that, several other machines tortured her muscles. As she finally limped back to the dorm, Rita was certain she would never walk normally again.

But while she was brushing her hair, Rita noticed the healthy, rosy color in her cheeks. "Hey, not bad," she thought.

Rowena laughed. "That's what fresh air and exercise can do for you, Murray. Come on, time for breakfast!"

"But I told you that I'm on a—" Then Rita remembered that she had promised to give up the diet. "I, uh— don't eat breakfast," she said.

"*Nonsense.* Breakfast is the most important meal of the day," Rowena said cheerfully. "Come on! I'll jog to the cafeteria with you. It'll do you good!"

An hour later, Rita returned to the dorm. On her way up to her room, she noticed that several other students, including Bambi, were just getting up.

"Wow! And here I am, ready to crack the books," Rita thought. "This isn't so bad. But there's no way I'm going to make of habit of it!"

For the rest of the morning, Rita studied. A few hours later, Rowena insisted that Rita eat a healthy lunch. Then it was back to the books.

By midafternoon, Rita's noble feelings were beginning to wear thin. She was getting a little annoyed with Rowena's efforts to whip her into shape.

"Take a break," Rowena told her. "You've worked hard, and you deserve some relaxation."

"Thanks a lot," Rita grumbled. "By the way, I'm going out with Gary this evening. So you get the night off, okay?"

"You're only having dinner with

Gary," Rowena said. "You should be home by nine, Rita."

Rita's eyes widened. She stared at Rowena in mute fury. "I should be *what*?" she asked in clipped tones. "Just who do you think you are?"

"You know," Rowena said, "I'm *you*. Remember?"

"I remember that I created you to help me play a game. But the game is over. Now it's time for you to leave."

"I can't," Rowena said with a smile. "You need me. It's almost time for you to get ready for your dinner date."

Rita's mouth tightened into a thin line. "I'll come home tonight when I'm good and ready, Rowena. Who knows? It may be at nine tonight or it may be at nine in the morning!"

"I don't think so," Rowena said. "You have to get a good night's sleep so you can be up bright and early."

"Oh, no!" Rita took two steps toward Rowena. "You are *not* waking me up at dawn again. I have a life outside the fitness center."

Rowena went on as if she hadn't heard a word. "It's getting late, Rita. You don't want to be late for your date with Gary." Then she vanished.

Rita muttered to herself angrily as she got dressed. But it was a great relief not to have the woman warrior peering over her shoulder. Before long, Rita's anger had faded away.

Rita took one last look at herself in the mirror. Not great—but not too bad, either. Of course her muscles were sore. If Gary suggested going dancing after dinner, Rita knew she'd have to say no. But maybe a movie would be nice.

The hallway was crowded with girls coming and going. As Rita reached the top of the stairs, she saw Bambi coming up. Bambi eyed Rita closely and then whistled in mock appreciation. Rita heard several other girls laugh. "Well, look at you all dressed up," Bambi said sarcastically. "Got a hot date, Rita?"

Rita felt the color rise in her cheeks. She had learned long ago not to respond to Bambi. So now she just smiled and started down the stairs.

"Hey, don't think that you can just ignore me, you ugly cow," Bambi snapped in a hard, cold voice. Suddenly Rita felt a stab of fear. Bambi's tone had turned vicious.

Out of the corner of her eye, Rita saw Bambi's arm shoot out. Rita gasped and pulled back. But before the cheerleader could touch her, the girl's arm suddenly froze in midair. In a flash, the look on her face changed from anger to fear, and she cried out—as if in pain. Then, as Rita watched in horror, Bambi flew across the staircase and was pinned against the banister!

"*You!* How d-d-dare you!" Bambi stuttered. The girls who had been with Bambi were looking on with shocked expressions on their faces.

"Go on, Rita!" The words seemed to echo on the staircase—but Rita knew that only she could hear them. She scurried down the stairs. As she reached the bottom she heard Bambi's voice.

"She *pushed* me! You saw her, didn't you? I could have been hurt. I'll get her for that!"

Then one of the little redhead's friends said, "But Bambi—Rita never touched you!"

# Chapter 6

"Earth to Murray. Come in, Murray."

Rita blinked and tried to focus her thoughts. Gary was gazing at her from across the restaurant table. She grinned, feeling embarrassed. "Uh, sorry."

"Oh, that's okay," Gary said. "I know I'm boring—"

"You are *not* boring," Rita exclaimed. "It's just—well, it's been a long day."

Gary took a bite of cheesecake. "You sure you don't want some of this?"

Rita shook her head. The cheesecake looked delicious, but a convincing little voice was now reminding her of what she could and could not eat.

"And not so little, that voice," Rita thought. As if in answer, she heard a mocking chuckle. Rita stifled a yawn. It wasn't even eight o'clock and she was already tired. "It's not the company," she said with a smile. "It's—"

Then suddenly, Rita found herself telling Gary all about her morning workout in the fitness room. Gary stared at her. "Sorry, could you say that again? I could have sworn I heard you use that forbidden word 'exercise.'"

If they hadn't been in such a nice restaurant, Rita would have thrown the salt shaker at him. "Very funny," she grumbled. "You told me to quit the diet. I have to do *something* to lose some of this weight!"

Gary shook his head in amazement. "But this is so *unlike* you, Murray!"

If he only knew, she thought. "Tell me some more about that article you're writing," she said.

Gary shook his head. "See what I mean? You never cared a hoot about computers and that kind of stuff before. What's up with you?"

Rita flashed him a smile. "Come on, Gary, here's your big chance to educate me. I know I need to learn a lot more about computers, and who better to teach me than you?"

She settled back to listen, happy to have Gary do the talking. It gave her a chance to mentally chew over her run-in with Bambi.

Rita was more than relieved that Rowena had kept Bambi from pushing her around. Bambi wouldn't have cared if Rita had ended up with a broken neck at the foot of the stairs. But now Rita was afraid that Bambi would *really* be out to get her!

"What if Rowena isn't around when Bambi tries it again?" Rita thought. She considered what else she could do. She could report the run-in to campus security. But how could she be sure that Bambi's friends would tell the truth? Would they admit that Bambi had started it? Rita was almost certain they would lie about it to protect their friend.

For a minute Rita even thought about moving out of the dorm. But that meant looking for a place off campus, and Rita really liked living in the dorm.

"You can't run away," the familiar voice whispered. "There will always be a Bambi out there to challenge you."

"You got a better idea?" Without thinking, Rita had spoken out loud.

"I beg your pardon?" Gary looked puzzled.

"Uh—" She took a drink of water to cover her confusion. "I thought you suggested we go for a walk."

Gary's frown deepened and became a look of concern. "No, I said nothing of the kind. I was talking about the use of computers in industry."

Rita's answering laugh was shrill. "I probably need to get my hearing checked. But speaking of leaving— maybe this is a good time."

When they were out on the street,

Gary said, "You want to catch a movie?"

"That sounds like . . ." Rita started to say before she saw Rowena standing just behind Gary. ". . . like a good idea for another time," she ended lamely. "I think I'll take a rain check, if you don't mind. I'm really beat tonight."

To her great relief, Gary was very understanding. "Sure—especially if you're getting up at dawn to go exercise. Good for you, Murray! I'm impressed. Maybe I'll join you sometime."

Rita smiled. "That would be great!"

"See," Rowena whispered. "You wanted to change your image, and now you're doing it. Okay, Murray, time to get back to the dorm so the pumpkin can change into a princess!"

"You've got your fairy stories mixed up," Rita blurted out.

Gary raised an eyebrow and blinked. "I beg your pardon?"

Rita groaned. When would she learn to keep her mouth shut? "I guess my brain kind of short circuits once in a while," she told him with a sigh. "Don't mind me, Gary!"

Thank goodness her old friend was in a forgiving mood.

And thank goodness Bambi wasn't around when Rita got back to the dorm. But that didn't mean she wouldn't be a problem tomorrow or the next day.

"I wonder if I ought to learn some of that self-defense stuff," Rita thought as she climbed into bed.

"Don't worry. You don't need self-defense as long as you've got me," Rowena answered. "I'll take good care of you, Rita."

At first Rowena's assurances seemed comforting. But as she drifted off to sleep, Rita felt a very *uncomfortable* thought poking at the back of her mind. Something that Rowena had said wasn't *right* somehow. But before she could pin down exactly what was wrong, Rita drifted off to sleep.

Chapter 7

"Rowena would make a great drill sergeant," Rita grumbled to herself as she plodded along on the treadmill.

The warrior woman had kept Rita on a tight rein for days. But at the same time, much as she hated to admit it, Rita *liked* the results. She had more energy now, and she felt a lot better. Best of all, the waistbands on some of her clothes were now getting loose.

"Get on the bicycle now, Murray," Rowena urged. "Enjoy yourself. A good attitude and self-discipline are both important parts of the workout."

Rita groaned. *Enjoy* yourself? It was pretty hard to have a good attitude when you felt like someone's slave!

And Rowena was becoming more

impatient every day. Once, when Rita hadn't moved fast enough, Rowena pushed her. It caught her off-guard and Rita landed on her face! Everyone in the room probably thought that she was just clumsy. But Rita was alarmed. Rowena's behavior was getting *scary*!

After breakfast, Rita headed for the library. For some reason, Rowena never went there. "Maybe she's figured out that reading is fat-free," Rita thought. "She knows I'm not likely to be attacked by an angry bookworm."

Rita found herself looking forward to her study sessions in the library. That was the one place where she could be absolutely sure that Rowena wasn't reading her thoughts.

Before she settled down to read, Rita checked the stacks. Were there any books on Tibet she might have missed? She came across one that had recently been shelved. This book covered the cultural beliefs of Tibetans.

Rita scanned the pages. She was more interested in native art, but cultural beliefs were part of art.

Then all of a sudden, two words seemed to leap out at Rita from the middle of a page: *mind creatures*. She blinked in surprise. This sounded interesting.

Tibetans believed that certain people could create a mind creature just by imagining that person. The Tibetan word for such a mind creature was *tulpa*. It wasn't all that simple, of course. The person who wanted to create a tulpa had to work very hard at it. The creator had to deliberately picture the mind creature until the image of the tulpa became crystal clear.

The book even gave an example. One woman had created a tulpa just to see if she could do it. It took many weeks, but she was successful. The creature she created was a friendly little man that could be seen by other people as well.

As time went by, however, the tulpa started to change both his looks and his attitude *on his own*. Instead of being a cheerful, round-faced person, he became lean and mean. At last the woman decided she had to get rid of him. But that was easier said than done. It took the woman six months of intense effort to destroy what she had created.

Rita shivered. "Good grief! Is that what I've created?" she wondered. "Is Rowena a tulpa?"

She remembered saying over and over that she had to change her image. Well, she certainly had done that. Also, Rowena had appeared at a time when Rita was on that crazy diet. "Maybe my *brain* was affected by the diet, too," Rita thought in horror. "I remember that I couldn't focus. I kept hearing things."

Rita reread the section on mind creatures. "At least no one else can *see* Rowena," she thought. "Maybe I haven't created a real tulpa after all."

She glanced at the clock and saw that it was time to eat lunch. She knew she didn't dare miss lunch. Rowena would have her hide! "Three salads a day keeps the doctor away," Rita grumbled as she put the book back on the shelf.

Rowena was waiting for Rita on the steps of the library. For the first time, Rita noticed something a little different about her. She no longer had softly rounded cheeks. Somehow, the lines in Rowena's face had hardened. Her body seemed even leaner and more muscular than before. And she no longer had a pretty smile. When she was amused now, her mouth twisted into a smirk that was anything but pretty.

"Hurry up, Murray—before the line gets too long in the cafeteria," Rowena snapped.

"Chill, Rowena," Rita thought.

In a split second Rowena's arm shot out. Caught off guard, Rita staggered under the blow. But just before she fell,

Rowena caught Rita's arm and helped her stay on her feet.

Rita's heart was pounding. She knew how it must have looked to the students around her. She felt embarrassed—but there was no possible way to explain it.

Rita caught the broad smile on Rowena's face just before the warrior woman vanished. Rita felt a wave of anger rising within her. She started to walk away, staring straight ahead. She pretended she couldn't hear the other students talking about her.

Then one of the students just behind her said something. Her words made Rita feel cold and a bit dizzy.

"Didn't you see what happened? That other girl *pushed* her!"

Chapter 8

Someone else had seen Rowena!

Rita bent down and pretended to tie her shoe, so she could listen to the rest of the conversation.

"What are you talking about? She wasn't pushed!"

"I saw it happen with my own eyes. It was a dark-haired girl—tall, thin. I only caught a glimpse of her."

"Are you *sure*? Maybe you saw a shadow. That must have been what it was. Just a shadow."

The voices faded as the students walked away. Rita took a deep breath, straightened up, and continued on to the cafeteria.

She forced her mind to remain as blank as possible. "What kind of dressing do you want on your salad?" she asked herself.

"How about some of those tasty wheat crackers with cottage cheese on the side?"

But new fears were now lurking beneath any thoughts of lunch. Still, Rita was determined not to let herself think about them. Not as long as she was outside the safety of the library.

An hour later, she was back in the library stacks and able to think freely. Rita decided that if people were starting to see Rowena, she *must* be a tulpa. Everything that was happening was exactly what the book had described. Rowena was changing from a fun-loving pal into a terrible tyrant!

"Which means I have to figure out some way to get rid of her," Rita said out loud.

She heard a sudden intake of breath and peered through the row of books on the shelf. Bambi was standing on the other side of the bookcase! The cheerleader was studying Rita with an odd expression on her face. As they stood there, silently staring at each other, Rita suddenly realized that Bambi had overheard what she had said.

"She thinks I'm going to get rid of a real person," Rita thought in dismay. "But I'm not a killer! I'm not a—"

Then the humor of the situation hit her. Maybe this was what it would take to make Bambi back off and leave her alone. If that was the case, so be it! Rita glared at Bambi and snarled. "What're you looking at? You want to be next on my hit list?"

Bambi gave a frightened squeak and scurried off as Rita smothered her laughter. Wasn't that always the way with bullies! They could only scare someone who was foolish enough to be afraid of them.

Rita thought about her problems with Rowena. If only it were that easy to get rid of a warrior woman!

Then suddenly Rita remembered what had been bugging her. Rowena's exact words had been: *"You don't need self-defense as long as you've got me. I'll take good care of you, Rita."*

In the beginning, Rita had enjoyed having Rowena take care of her. "But that was only because I was lazy," Rita thought. "I always knew how to get in better shape. It was just too much trouble."

Now Rita thought about how she had slowly let Rowena take control of her life. She picked up her pen and began to doodle. Then she looked down at what she'd drawn. Rita was surprised, but also pleased. She'd drawn herself again—but this time she'd drawn herself the way she actually looked. She was still too heavy, of course. And her short hair didn't swirl out in a silky curtain the way Rowena's did. But at the same time, Rita could see very clearly how much she was changing for the better.

"Hmmm. It seems that the more I change, the more Rowena tries to control me," Rita thought to herself.

That was it! Suddenly Rita knew how she could regain control of her own life. She grabbed her backpack and headed for the door. Now Rita was excited as well as scared. If her plan worked, she'd be free of Rowena and back in control.

As she hurried from the library, Rita thought about the risk she was taking. After all, Rowena was mighty strong.

"Just remember," she thought to herself, "the secret is not just muscle."

"What secret?" Rowena sounded impatient.

Rita hesitated, but kept on walking. She could feel Rowena next to her.

"I said, *what secret?*"

"I'm thinking about my paper on Tibet," Rita thought. "I need the secret to writing a good paper."

She could feel Rowena's anger. "Rita, why are you lying to me?"

"What makes you think I'm lying?" Rita thought.

"I can see the color of the lie."

"And what color would that be?" Rita asked innocently.

"Don't change the subject," Rowena snapped. "What secret?"

Rita sighed. "The secret of getting

Gary to pay more attention to me."

Rowena frowned. "The secret of—no, that is also a lie."

"Okay, then *you* figure it out," Rita thought. She walked faster.

"Rita, don't play games with me!" Rowena grabbed Rita's backpack and tugged. Rita's arms beat the air as she fought to keep her balance. Then, just as she was sure that she was going to fall backwards, Rowena steadied her.

"You *must* do as I say," Rowena said. "I will take good care of you, Rita, but you must do what I tell you to do. And you must answer all my questions."

"I wonder what happened to that cool chick I met in the Virtual Reality booth?" Rita thought. "Remember her? She was a lot of fun, a real partner."

Rowena's eyes narrowed. Up close, Rita could see how much Rowena had changed in just the last few hours.

"Rowena, I don't *want* you to take care of me," Rita thought calmly. "I'm an adult, and I can take care of myself."

Rowena's mouth tightened. "You *know* you don't do a good job of taking care of yourself, Rita. Why, if I hadn't been taking care of you—"

"Hold on! You've *changed*," Rita cut in. "But that's okay, because so have I. You showed me how to become a new person, Rowena. I admit that it was hard at first—but I'm getting to like the new me." She grinned. "So you see, Rowena, I no longer *need* to have you take care of me. You can go away now."

Rowena bared her teeth in an agly scowl. *"I don't think so, Rita!* Do you remember the night Bambi tried to push you down the stairs? Have you forgotten what I did to her?"

Rita shook her head.

"Well, I can do it to *you*, too!"

Rita stared at the tulpa in horror. How had such a thing happened? Her wonderful dream creature had become her worst nightmare!

Chapter 9

When her alarm clock went off the next morning, Rita didn't have to look to know what time it was. She'd set the alarm for 4:30. Rita wasn't sure where Rowena spent the night, but she always appeared at the stroke of 5:00.

As tired as she was, Rita pulled on her sweats. She knew what would happen. When Rowena discovered that Rita was gone, she'd certainly come looking for her. But Rita was very determined. She knew she had to follow the plan she'd come up with the day before. It was her only hope!

Rita reached the fitness center just as it was opening up. One or two other sleepy-eyed students went in at the same time. Rita headed for a bank of pay phones in the entryway to call Gary.

The phone in Gary's room rang again and again, but no one answered.

"Come on, Gary, pick up!" Rita muttered. She glanced at her watch. Then she heard the receiver being lifted—and dropped. Finally, she heard Gary's hoarse greeting. "Hello?"

"Gary, it's me, Rita!" It took her a while to convince him that her call was no prank.

Finally, he agreed to meet her a little later in the library. "Although I think you're nuts," he grumbled. "Sane people don't get up at—"

"Talk to you later," Rita said just before hanging up.

Rita pedaled the stationary bike as she tried to figure out why Rowena wanted to run her life. "Every day she gets stronger," Rita thought. "And now other people can see her."

In the past few days, people had often confused the two women. That's what helped Rita to make up her mind.

It was clear there was simply no room in this world for *two* of her!

"Maybe Rowena could have a life of her own, if only—"

Rita froze. That was it! "She's *afraid* of what will happen to her if I no longer need her," Rita realized.

Rita met Gary at the library a few hours later. He had a rumpled look, as if he'd just gotten up. "This had better be good," he grumbled. "I don't create computer games for just anyone."

In order to convince him to create a new game, Rita had to explain about Rowena. She tried to keep it simple.

"Rowena is a new girl on campus. She seems to think that being better than everyone else means being stronger— you know, more athletic. I want her to see that there are other ways for people to be winners."

Gary listened closely to everything Rita had to say. Then he gave a low whistle and looked at her in admiration.

"You have an interesting mind, Murray," he said. "I like your idea! You'll have to give me a couple of days to work on this, though. Deal?"

Rita nodded. Then, just as she was leaving, she turned back to smile at Gary. "I was wrong before," she said softly. "You really *are* a hero, Gary!"

Gary's face turned bright red.

Two days later, Gary telephoned Rita. He said that she and Rowena should meet him at the Triple-E shop. "I've arranged to have a booth set aside for you and your friend."

Rita's heart began to pound. "The game is really special, right?"

Gary chuckled. "It's a good thing the Triple-E guys seem to like me so much," he said. "They thought the whole thing sounded kind of crazy—but they were willing to give it a try. And oh, yeah, this game is *very* special."

Rita knew that the moment she headed for the mall, Rowena would find her. And sure enough, Rita's mind creature quickly fell into step. "Where are you going?" Rowena demanded.

Rita explained that she was going to the Triple-E shop. "That's where you and I first met," she said.

"I know that," Rowena snapped. "But why are we going back?"

"To play a new game," Rita said.

Rowena was silent for a moment. Then she said, "This sounds very foolish, Rita. We both know that I'm better at these games than you are."

"Look, Gary created this game and I told him we'd test it," Rita explained. Then, after a moment, she added, "And listen, Rowena—maybe I'm better than you think I am."

When they got to the Triple-E shop, Gary was waiting. He gave Rowena an admiring glance as Rita introduced them.

Rowena paid no attention to Gary. "You can't win, Rita," she said crossly. "You have more important things to do

—clothes to iron, a test to study for—"

"Hey!" Gary exclaimed. "Ease up, Rowena. Rita needs to have some fun now and then."

Rowena glared at Gary. But behind the anger Rita saw a look of naked fear in her mind creature's eyes. The warrior woman was losing control—and she knew it!

"I know for sure I can win this one," Rita thought, "but will Rowena lose gracefully?"

"I do not lose," Rowena snapped.

While they were putting on the electronic gear, Rita turned to Rowena. "Let's make a bet, Rowena. If I lose, I won't fight you anymore. If you win, I'll do just what you tell me to do. But if I win—you have to go back where you came from."

Rowena froze. "What do you mean?"

"You told me once that you were part of me, part of my mind," Rita said.

"But if I have to go back, I'll—I'll no

longer be *me*," Rowena said with more than a little fear in her voice.

"So you don't think you can win Gary's new game?" Rita asked.

Rowena snarled. "Of course I will win." She raised her arm and clenched her fist to show Rita the rippling muscles. "It's a bet!"

"Let the game begin!" Rita cried out.

A second or two later they found themselves standing in the middle of an arena. Rita looked around. The stands were crowded with virtual reality people who had come to cheer the contestants. At any moment, Rita expected to see a football team or a team of Roman gladiators run onto the playing field.

She glanced at Rowena. The warrior woman smiled. Clearly, she had no doubt that her superior strength would make her the winner. "I hope Gary didn't misunderstand what I need here," Rita thought nervously.

Then suddenly one of the gates in the

wall opened. A man wearing a three-piece suit walked to the middle of the arena. Holding a microphone in one hand, he raised his arms over his head, smiling at the crowd. The people in the stands roared with wild anticipation. Rowena looked puzzled.

"The first contestant will choose a category," the man said. "Rita Murray, what is your category?"

"I choose Tibet," Rita called out in a clear, loud voice.

Rowena looked bewildered. "Who is that man?" she asked. "What kind of game is this?"

"He's the quiz master," Rita said. Her voice was shaking, but she forced herself to stand tall. "And this is a game of wits, Rowena—a battle of brains."

Rowena stared at Rita in stunned silence.

"Well, Miss Murray? Are you ready for the first question in your chosen category?" the quiz master asked.

"I'm ready," Rita answered.

"But—but I don't know anything about Tibet," Rowena complained.

"Then I'm afraid you're going to lose," Rita said. She turned to the quiz master. "What's the question?"

"Tibet is located on a high plateau north of what mountains?" the quiz master called out.

"The Himalayas!" Rita shouted. The crowd roared.

"Correct!" called out the smiling quiz master. "Now, name Tibet's capital city."

Rowena gasped. "This is not fair!" In fury and frustration, the warrior woman pulled her sword from its sheath. She took an angry step toward Rita.

Rita started to move away, but then she stopped and held her ground. "Lhasa is the capital city," she said calmly. The crowd went wild.

"I'm winning," Rita said to Rowena. "So play fair. Why don't you just admit it? It's time to go back where you came from."

Rowena gave a wild cry. She leaped toward Rita, waving the sword over her head. Rita sucked in her breath. She was absolutely terrified. But she had made up her mind that she would never give in to Rowena again.

Then Rita realized that she could see the far wall right through Rowena's body. The warrior woman was fading!

"Don't worry, Rowena. When you're part of me again, we will both be stronger and better," Rita said softly. "After all, we're two parts of the same person. I need you as much as you need me."

Rowena was now only a pale shadow, yet Rita could tell that she was still unwilling to give up.

"You did your job, Rowena. Look at everything I learned from you," Rita went on. "You taught me self-discipline and courage. You showed me how to walk tall and be proud of myself."

The warrior woman gazed at her weakly, and Rita almost felt sorry for her. "Think about it, Rowena," Rita said gently. "*Together* we will make one dynamic woman!"

Then, Rowena suddenly disappeared. Rita waited, holding her breath. She turned slowly, looking all around. Rowena was nowhere in sight. Then Rita said the warrior woman's name softly. No one answered.

Rita took a long, deep breath. The nightmare was over. When she stepped out of the game booth, she found Gary waiting. "Well?" he demanded. "What happened?"

Rita smiled. "I won! That was really a fantastic game, Gary. You ought to put it on the market."

Gary looked at her thoughtfully. "Huh? A game that doesn't rely on violence, but challenges the players to use their heads? I don't know, Murray. You think it might catch on?"

"It just might. What have you got to lose?" she asked. "Come on, Gary, this time I'll buy *you* dinner."

As they headed for the entrance, Gary said. "Speaking of losing, what happened to your gal pal?"

"Rowena?" Rita smiled. "I guess she split. She must have slipped out of the booth when no one was looking."

"Too ashamed to face me, huh?" Gary said with a laugh. "It's just as well she's gone because—" He gasped.

Rita glanced over at him in alarm. "What's wrong?"

Gary blinked. "Sorry! I guess I may need some new glasses. Just now I looked into your eyes, and for a moment—" He shook his head. "Nah. You're going to think I'm nuts."

"I doubt it," Rita said. "Tell me what you saw."

Gary wriggled uncomfortably. "I could have sworn I saw Rowena!"

COMPREHENSION QUESTIONS

RECALL

1. What bad habit did Rita want to break?

2. What was Gary eager to try out at the Triple-E store?

3. In what campus building was Rita safe from Rowena?

4. Why did Rita say she named her mind creature Rowena?

WHO DID WHAT?

1. Which character called Rita an "ugly cow"?

2. Which character invited Rita out for a hot fudge sundae?

3. Which character wore a black suede outfit with thigh-high boots?

4. Which character named the capital city of Tibet?

INFERENCE

1. Why did Rita think she was "hearing things" when Rowena first spoke to her?

2. At the end of the story, why did Rita want to get rid of Rowena?

VOCABULARY

1. What is the Tibetan word for a creature like Rowena?

2. Rowena called Rita a *wimp*. What is a wimp?

NOTING DETAILS

1. The virtual reality game sent Rita and Rowena on a quest. Who did they have to rescue?

2. What threat did Rowena make when Rita said she no longer needed her?